LITTLE MISS
NEAT
Cleans Up

Original concept by Roger Hargreaves
Illustrated and written by Adam Hargreaves

MR. MEN   LITTLE MISS

MR. MEN™ LITTLE MISS™ © THOIP (a SANRIO company)

Little Miss Neat Cleans Up © 2014 THOIP (a Sanrio company)
Printed and published under licence from Price Stern Sloan, Inc., Los Angeles.
First published in France 1997 by Hachette Livre
This edition published in 2015 by Dean, an imprint of Egmont UK Limited,
The Yellow Building, 1 Nicholas Road, London W11 4AN

ISBN 978 0 6035 7198 5
63578/1
Printed in Great Britain

All rights reserved. No part of this publication may be reproduced, stored in a retrieval system, or transmitted,
in any form or by any means, electronic, mechanical, photocopying, recording or otherwise,
without the prior permission of the publisher and copyright owner.

Just like every other day, Little Miss Neat had tidied her house from top to bottom.

But today she was expecting a guest, so she wanted Twopin Cottage to be as neat as two pins!

Ring!

"Hello, Mr Clumsy," said Little Miss Neat, opening the door. "Do come in, but be careful of the floor polisher."

But, oh dear, Mr Clumsy immediately bumped into the floor polisher, only just managing to catch the cake tin he had brought with him.

"I've brought you a chocolate cream cake," he said proudly, trying to open the tin.

He pulled at the lid. But it wouldn't come off. He pulled again. He pulled again and again, and finally the lid flew off the tin and …

… the chocolate cream flew across the room and landed with a SPLAT! on the beautiful wallpaper that Little Miss Neat was so proud of.

Mr Clumsy was so sorry for the mess he had made.

"Do let me help you hang new wallpaper," he said, helpfully.

The thought of Mr Clumsy inside her neat little house with a ladder and wallpaper paste was too much for Little Miss Neat.

She refused, thanked him for his offer, and hurried him out of the door as quickly as she could!

For the rest of that day, Little Miss Neat
rubbed and scrubbed and rubbed some more.

No matter how hard she tried, the marks just
wouldn't come off the wallpaper.

She ran to the hardware shop.

"I've just what you need," said the man in the shop. "With Clever Clean, the miracle cleaner, your marks will be gone in no time at all."

Little Miss Neat rubbed and she scrubbed. She scrubbed and she rubbed all through the night.

But it was no good, even with Clever Clean, the miracle cleaner, she couldn't get rid of the chocolaty marks.

Little Miss Neat didn't know what to do.

The next morning, she rang Mr Fussy.

"Please can you come as quickly as possible?" she said. "I've spent all night trying to clean the marks that Mr Clumsy made on my walls, but I can't get rid of them."

As soon as Mr Fussy arrived, Little Miss Neat showed him the terrible marks on the wall.

"But your wallpaper is perfect," said an astonished Mr Fussy. "I've never seen such clean wallpaper. You should be awarded a silver medal for cleanliness. And I, of course, would get the gold!"

"But what about all those marks?" exclaimed Little Miss Neat. "All over the walls!"

"Hmm. If you wouldn't mind showing me your glasses for a moment," asked Mr Fussy.

Can you see what the problem was with Little Miss Neat's glasses?

"All the marks have gone!" said Little Miss Neat, as she took off her glasses. "It's quite extraordinary!"

Now all that Little Miss Neat could see were the pretty flowers on her wallpaper.

And every last flower was perfectly clean!

She put on her glasses again, and once more the wallpaper was covered in chocolaty marks.

Then suddenly, red with embarrassment, she realised her mistake and cried:

"I see! It's my glasses that are dirty, not the walls. Oh, to think that I hadn't cleaned my glasses! How terrible!"

Just then they heard a ring.

There was somebody at the door.

That somebody was Mr Clumsy carrying a bunch of flowers.

"Hello, Little Miss Neat," he said. "I've come to say sorry for my terrible clumsiness yesterday."

"Do come in," said Little Miss Neat, kindly. "I'll put these pretty flowers in a nice, clean vase, with perfectly clear water and give you a very neat slice of cake."

But no sooner had Mr Clumsy walked in the door than he stepped into the bucket that Little Miss Neat had been using for her cleaning. The water splashed all over Little Miss Neat and Mr Fussy.

They were soaked from head to toe!

"Back to work, Little Miss Neat," laughed Mr Fussy.

"Oh, I am so terribly sorry," said Mr Clumsy.

"I'm starting to get used to your clumsiness, Mr Clumsy!" giggled Little Miss Neat. "In fact, I must thank you …

… My glasses are now perfectly clean again!"